Winnie -the- Pooh

Story Treasury

Adapted from the Stories by A. A. Milne

Pooh

First published in Great Britain 1999
by Methuen Children's Books
an imprint of Egmont Children's Books Limited
239 Kensington High Street, London W8 6SA
Copyright © 1999 Michael John Brown, Peter Janson-Smith,
Roger Hugh Vaughan Charles Morgan and Timothy Michael Robinson,
Trustees of the Pooh Properties.
Published under license from The Walt Disney Company.
Adapted from *Winnie-the-Pooh*, first published 1926
and *The House at Pooh Corner*, first published 1928
text by A. A. Milne and line drawings by E. H. Shepard
copyright under the Berne Convention.
New and adapted line drawings and colouring of the illustrations by Stuart Trotter
Book design by Daniel Devlin
copyright © 1999 Egmont Children's Books Limited
ISBN 0 416 19759 0
Printed and bound in Spain

1 3 5 7 9 10 8 6 4 2

Contents

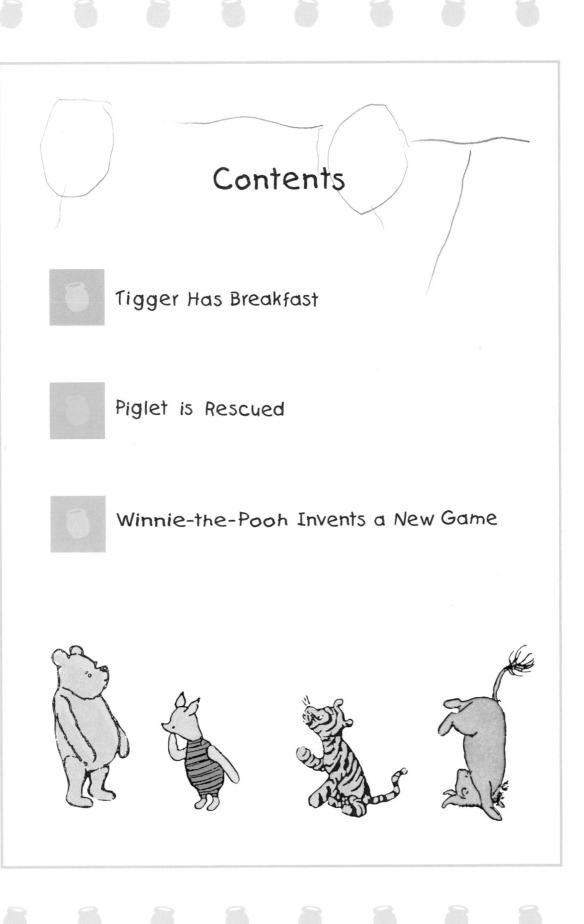

Tigger
Has
Breakfast

Adapted from the Stories by A. A. Milne

Winnie-the-Pooh woke up suddenly in the middle of the night and listened. He got out of bed, lit his candle, and went to see if anybody was trying to get into his honey-cupboard. They weren't so he got back into bed. Then he heard the noise again.

"Is that you, Piglet?" he said.

But it wasn't.

The noise went on.

"*Worraworraworraworraworra,*" it said.

"There are lots of noises in the Forest, but this is different," thought Pooh. "It isn't a growl, and it isn't a purr, but it's a noise of some kind, made by a strange animal! I shall get up and ask him not to do it."

He got out of bed and opened his front door.

"Hallo!" said Pooh.

"Hallo!" said Whatever-it-was.

"Who is it?" Pooh asked.

"Me," said the strange voice.

In the candle-light, Whatever-it-was and Pooh looked at each other.

"I'm Pooh," said Pooh.

"I'm Tigger," said Tigger.

Pooh had never seen an animal like this before. "Does Christopher Robin know about you?"

"Of course he does," said Tigger.

"Well," said Pooh, "it's the middle of the night which is a good time for going to sleep. Tomorrow morning we'll have some honey for breakfast. Do Tiggers like honey?"

"They like everything," said Tigger cheerfully.

"Then if they like going to sleep on the floor, I'll go back to bed," said Pooh, "and we'll do things in the morning. Good night."

And he got back into bed and went fast asleep.

In the morning, the first thing Pooh saw was Tigger, sitting in front of the mirror, looking at himself.

"I've found somebody just like me. I thought I was the only one of them," said Tigger.

Pooh began to explain what a mirror was, but just as he was getting to the interesting part, Tigger said:

"Excuse me a moment, but there's something climbing up your table," and with one loud "*Worraworraworraworraworra*" he leapt up and pulled the tablecloth to the ground. After a terrible struggle, he said: "Have I won?"

"That's my tablecloth," said Pooh, as he began to unwind Tigger.

"I wondered what it was," said Tigger.

"It goes on the table and you put things on it."

"Then why did it try to bite me when I wasn't looking?"

"It didn't," said Pooh.

Pooh put the cloth back on the table, placed a honey-pot on the cloth, and they sat down to breakfast.

Tigger took a large mouthful of honey. He looked up at the ceiling with his head on one side, and made exploring noises with his tongue … and then he said:

"Tiggers don't like honey."

"Oh!" said Pooh, trying to sound sad. Pooh felt rather pleased about this, and said that when he had finished his own breakfast, he would take Tigger round to Piglet's house, and Tigger could try some haycorns.

"Thank you, Pooh, because haycorns are really what Tiggers like best."

Off they set and Pooh explained as they went that Piglet was a Very Small Animal who didn't like bouncing, and asked Tigger not to be too Bouncy at first.

Tigger said that Tiggers were only bouncy before breakfast, and that as soon as they had had a few haycorns they became Quiet and Refined.

They knocked on the door of Piglet's house.

"Hallo, Piglet. This is Tigger."

"Oh, is it?" said Piglet. "I thought Tiggers were smaller than that."

"Not the big ones," said Tigger.

"They like haycorns," said Pooh, "so that's what we've come for, because poor Tigger hasn't had any breakfast yet."

"Help yourself," said Piglet.

After a long munching noise Tigger said:

"Ee-ers o i a-ors."

Then he said: "Skoos ee," and went outside.

When he came back in he said: "Tiggers don't like haycorns."

"But you said they liked everything except honey," said Pooh.

"Everything except honey *and* haycorns," explained Tigger.

Piglet, who was rather glad that Tiggers didn't like haycorns, said, "What about thistles?"

"Thistles," said Tigger, "are what Tiggers like best."

So the three of them set off to find Eeyore.

"Hallo, Eeyore!" said Pooh. "This is Tigger."

"What is?" said Eeyore.

"This," explained Pooh and Piglet together. Tigger smiled.

"He's just come," explained Piglet.

Eeyore thought for a long time and then said: "When is he going?"

Pooh explained that Tigger was a great friend of Christopher Robin's, who had come to stay in the Forest; and Piglet explained to Tigger that he mustn't mind what Eeyore said because he was *always* gloomy; and Tigger explained to anybody who was listening that he hadn't had any breakfast yet.

"I knew there was something," said Pooh. "That was why we came to see you, Eeyore."

"Then come this way, Tigger," said Eeyore.

Eeyore led the way to a patch of thistles, and waved a hoof at it.

"A little patch I was keeping for my birthday," he said, "but what *are* birthdays? Help yourself, Tigger."

Tigger thanked him and looked at Pooh.

"Are these really thistles?" he whispered.

"Yes," said Pooh.

"What Tiggers like best?"

"That's right," said Pooh.

So Tigger took a large mouthful, and he gave a large crunch.

"*Ow!*" said Tigger.

He sat down and put his paw in his mouth.

"What's the matter?" asked Pooh.

"*Hot!*" mumbled Tigger.

He stopped shaking his head to get the prickles out, and explained that Tiggers didn't like thistles.

"But you *said* that Tiggers liked everything except honey and haycorns," said Pooh.

"*And* thistles," said Tigger, who was now running round in circles with his tongue hanging out.

Pooh looked at him sadly.

"What are we going to do?" he asked Piglet.

Piglet said at once that they must go and see Christopher Robin.

"You'll find him with Kanga," said Eeyore. He came close to Pooh, and said in a loud whisper:

"*Could* you ask your friend to do his exercises somewhere else? I shall be having lunch directly, and don't want it bounced on just before I begin. A trifling matter but we all have our little ways."

Pooh called to Tigger.

"Come along and we'll go and see Kanga. She's sure to have lots of breakfast for you."

Tigger rushed off, excitedly.

As Pooh and Piglet walked after him, Pooh thought of a poem:

What shall we do about
poor little Tigger?
If he never eats nothing
he'll never get bigger.
He doesn't like honey and
haycorns and thistles
Because of the taste and
because of the bristles.
And all the good things
which an animal likes
Have the wrong sort of swallow
or too many spikes.

"He's quite big enough anyhow," said Piglet.

Pooh thought about this, and then he murmured to himself:

But whatever his weight in pounds,
shillings, and ounces,
He always seems bigger because
of his bounces.

"And that's the poem," said Pooh. "Do you like it?"

"All except the shillings," said Piglet. "They oughtn't to be there."

"They wanted to come in after the pounds," explained Pooh, "so I let them. It is the best way to write poetry."

At last they came to Kanga's house, and there was Christopher Robin.

"Oh, there you are, Tigger!" said Christopher Robin. "I knew you'd be somewhere."

"I've been finding things in the Forest," said Tigger importantly. "I've found a pooh and a piglet and an eeyore, but I can't find any breakfast."

Pooh and Piglet explained what had happened.

"Don't *you* know what Tiggers like?" asked Pooh.

"I expect if I thought very hard I should," said Christopher Robin, "but I *thought* Tigger knew."

So they went into Kanga's house. They told Kanga what they wanted, and Kanga said very kindly, "Well, look in my cupboard, Tigger dear, and see what you'd like."

She knew at once that, however big Tigger seemed to be, he wanted as much kindness as Roo.

"Shall I look, too?" said Pooh, who was beginning to feel a little eleven o'clockish. And he found a small tin of condensed milk (that he thought Tiggers wouldn't like) and took it into a corner by itself.

But the more Tigger put his nose into this and his paw into that, the more things he found which Tiggers didn't like.

And when he had found everything in the cupboard, and couldn't eat any of it, he said to Kanga, "What happens now?"

But Kanga and Christopher Robin and Piglet were all watching Roo have his Extract of Malt. And Kanga was saying, "Now, Roo dear, you promised."

"What is it?" whispered Tigger to Piglet.

"His Strengthening Medicine," said Piglet. "He hates it."

So Tigger came closer, and he leant over the back of Roo's chair.

Then suddenly he put out his tongue, and took one large galollop, which made Kanga jump with surprise. "Oh!" she said, and then clutched at the spoon just as it was disappearing, and pulled it safely back out of Tigger's mouth. But the Extract of Malt had gone.

"He's taken my medicine, he's taken my medicine!" sang Roo happily.

Then Tigger looked up at the ceiling, and closed his eyes, and his tongue went round his chops, in case he had left any outside, and a peaceful smile came over his face as he said, "So *that's* what Tiggers like!"

Which explains why he always lived at Kanga's house afterwards, and had Extract of Malt for breakfast, dinner, and tea. And sometimes, when Kanga thought he wanted strengthening, he had a spoonful or two of Roo's breakfast after meals as medicine.

"But *I* think," said Piglet to Pooh, "that he's been strengthened quite enough."

Piglet
is
Rescued

Adapted from the Stories by A. A. Milne

It rained and it rained and it rained. Piglet told himself that never in all his life, never had he seen so much rain. Days and days and days.

"If only," he thought, as he looked out of the window, "I had been in Pooh's house, or Christopher Robin's house, or Rabbit's house when it began to rain, then I should have had Company all this time, instead of being here all alone, with nothing to do except wonder when it will stop."

And he imagined himself with Pooh, saying, "Did you ever see such rain, Pooh?" and Pooh saying, "Isn't it *awful*, Piglet?"

It would have been jolly to talk like this, and really, it wasn't much good having anything exciting like floods, if you couldn't share them with somebody.

For it was rather exciting. The little dry ditches in which Piglet had nosed about so often had become streams, the little streams across which he had splashed were rivers, and the river, between whose steep banks they had played so happily, had sprawled out of its own bed and was taking up so much room everywhere, that Piglet was beginning to wonder whether it would be coming into *his* bed soon.

"It's a little Anxious," he said to himself, "to be a Very Small Animal Entirely Surrounded by Water. And I can't do *anything*."

It went on raining, and every day the water got a little higher, until now it was nearly up to Piglet's window ... and he hadn't done anything.

Then suddenly he remembered a story which Christopher Robin had told him about a man on a desert island who had written something in a bottle and thrown it into the sea; and Piglet thought that if he wrote something in a bottle and threw it in the water, perhaps somebody would come and rescue *him!*

He left the window and began to search the house, and at last he found a pencil and a small piece of dry paper, and a bottle with a cork to it. And he wrote on one side of the paper:

HELP!
PIGLIT (ME)

and on the other side:

IT'S ME PIGLIT,
HELP HELP!

Then he put the paper in the bottle, and he
threw the bottle as far as he could throw and he
watched it floating slowly away in the distance.

When the rain began Pooh was asleep. It rained, and it rained, and it rained, and he slept, and he slept, and he slept. He had had a tiring day. You remember how he discovered the North Pole; well, he was so proud of this that he asked Christopher Robin if there were any other Poles such as a Bear of Little Brain might discover.

"There's a South Pole," said Christopher Robin, "and I expect there's an East Pole and a West Pole, though people don't like talking about them."

Then suddenly he was dreaming. He was at the East Pole, and it was a very cold pole with snow and ice all over it. He had found a beehive to sleep in, but there wasn't room for his legs, so he had left them outside. And Wild Woozles, such as inhabit the East Pole, came and nibbled all the fur off his legs to make Nests for their Young. And the more they nibbled, the colder his legs got, until suddenly he woke up with an *Ow!* – and there he was, sitting in his chair with his feet in the water, and water all round him!

He splashed to his door and looked out ...

"This is Serious," said Pooh. "I must have an Escape."

So he took his largest pot of honey and escaped with it to a broad branch of his tree, well above the water, and then he climbed down again and escaped with another pot ... and when the whole Escape was finished, there was Pooh sitting on his branch, dangling his legs, and there, beside him, were ten pots of honey ...

Two days later, there was Pooh, sitting on his
branch, dangling his legs, and there beside him,
were four pots of honey.

Three days later, there was Pooh, sitting on his
branch, dangling his legs, and there beside him,
was one pot of honey.

Four days later, there was Pooh …

And it was on the morning of the fourth day that Piglet's bottle come floating past him, and with one loud cry of "Honey!" Pooh plunged into the water, seized the bottle, and struggled back to his tree again.

"Bother!" said Pooh, as he opened it. "All that wet for nothing. What's that bit of paper doing?"

He took it out and looked.

"It's a Missage," he said to himself, "and I can't read it. I must find Christopher Robin or Owl or Piglet, and they will tell me what this message means. Only I can't swim. Bother!"

Then he had an idea.
He said to himself:
"If a bottle can float,
then a jar can float, and if a jar floats, I can sit on
the top of it, if it's a very big jar."

So he took his biggest jar,
and corked it up.

"All boats have to have a
name," he said, "so I shall call
mine *The Floating Bear*." And
with these words he dropped
his boat into
the water
and jumped
in after it.

Christopher Robin lived at the very top of the
Forest. It rained, and it rained, and it rained, but
the water couldn't come up to *his* house. It was
rather jolly to look down into the valleys and see
the water all round him, but it rained so hard that
he stayed indoors most of the time, and thought
about things.

Every morning he went out with his umbrella
and put a stick in the place where the water came
up to, and every next morning he went out and
couldn't see his stick any more, so he put another
stick in the place where the water came up to. On
the morning of the fifth day he saw the water all
round him, and knew that for the
first time in his life he was
on a real island.

It was on this morning that Owl came flying over the water to say "How do you do?" to his friend Christopher Robin.

"I say, Owl," said Christopher Robin, "isn't this fun? I'm on an island!"

"The atmospheric conditions have been very unfavourable lately," said Owl.

"The what?"

"It has been raining," Owl explained.

"Yes," said Christopher Robin. "It has. Have you seen Pooh?"

"Here I am," said a growly voice behind him. "Pooh!"

They rushed into each other's arms.

"How did you get here, Pooh?" asked Christopher Robin.

"On my boat," said Pooh proudly. "I had a Very Important Missage sent me in a bottle, and owing to having got some water in my eyes, I couldn't read it, so I brought it to you. On my boat."

With these proud words he gave Christopher Robin the missage.

"But it's from Piglet!" cried Christopher Robin when he had read it. "We must rescue him at once! Owl, could you rescue him on your back?"

"I don't think so," said Owl.

"Then would you fly to him at once and say the Rescue is Coming? And Pooh and I will think of a Rescue and come as quick as ever we can."

Owl, speechless for once, flew off.

"Now then, Pooh," said Christopher Robin, "where's your boat?"

"There!" said Pooh, pointing proudly to *The Floating Bear*.

It wasn't what Christopher Robin expected, and the more he looked at it, the more he thought what a Brave and Clever Bear Pooh was. Pooh looked modestly down his nose and tried to pretend he wasn't.

"But it's too small for two of us," said Christopher Robin sadly.

"Three of us with Piglet."

"That makes it smaller still. Oh, Pooh Bear, what shall we do?"

And then this Bear, Pooh Bear, said something so clever that Christopher Robin could only look at him with mouth open and eyes staring. "We might go in your umbrella," said Pooh.

For suddenly Christopher Robin saw that they might. He opened his umbrella and put it point downwards in the water. It floated but wobbled. Pooh got in.

He was just beginning to say that it was all right now, when he found that it wasn't. Then Christopher Robin got in, and it wobbled no longer.

You can imagine Piglet's joy when at last he saw the good ship *Brain of Pooh (Captain*, C. Robin; *1st Mate*, P. Bear), coming over the sea to rescue him …

And as that is really the end of the story, I think I shall stop there.

Winnie-the-Pooh
Invents a New Game

Adapted from the Stories by A. A. Milne

One day, as Pooh was walking towards the wooden bridge which crosses the river, he was trying to make up a piece of poetry about fir-cones, because there they were, lying about on each side of him, and he felt singy.

So he picked a fir-cone up, and looked at it, and said it himself, "This is a very good fir-cone, and something ought to be done with it." But he couldn't think of anything.

And then this came into his head suddenly:

Here is a myst'ry
About a little fir-tree
Owl says it's his tree
And Kanga says it's her tree

"Which doesn't make sense," said Pooh,
"because Kanga doesn't live in a tree."

He had just come to the bridge; and not looking
where he was going, he tripped over something, and
the fir-cone jerked out of his paw into the river.

"Bother," said Pooh, as it floated slowly under the bridge, and he went back to get another fir-cone which had a rhyme to it. But then he thought that he would just look at the river instead, because it was a peaceful sort of day, so he lay down and looked at it, and it slipped slowly away beneath him ... and suddenly, there was his fir-cone slipping away too.

"That's funny," said Pooh. "I dropped it on the other side," said Pooh, "and it came out on this side! I wonder if it would do it again?" And he went back for some more fir-cones.

It did. It kept on doing it. Then he dropped two in at once, and leant over the bridge to see which of them would come out first; and one of them did; but as they were both the same size, he didn't know if it was the one which he wanted to win, or the other one.

And that was the beginning of the game called Poohsticks, which Pooh invented, and which he and his friends used to play on the edge of the Forest. But they played with sticks instead of fir-cones, because they were easier to mark.

Now one day Pooh and Piglet and Rabbit and Roo were all playing Poohsticks together. They had dropped their sticks in when Rabbit said "Go!" and then they had hurried across to the other side of the bridge, and now they were all leaning over the edge, waiting to see whose stick would come out first.

"I can see mine!" cried Roo. "No, I can't, it's something else. Can you see yours, Piglet? I thought I could see mine, but I couldn't. There it is! No, it isn't. Can you see yours, Pooh?"

"No," said Pooh.

"Mine's a sort of greyish one," said Piglet, not daring to lean too far over in case he fell in.

"Yes, that's what I can see. It's coming over on to my side."

Rabbit leant over further than ever, looking for his, and Roo wriggled up and down, calling out "Come on, stick! Stick, stick, stick!" and Piglet got very excited because his was the only one which had been seen, and that meant that he was winning.

"It's coming!" said Pooh.

"Are you sure it's mine?" squeaked Piglet excitedly.

"Yes, because it's grey. A big grey one. Here it comes! A very – big – grey – Oh, no, it isn't, it's Eeyore."

And out floated Eeyore.

"Eeyore!" cried everybody.

Looking very calm, very dignified, with his legs in the air, came Eeyore from beneath the bridge.

"It's Eeyore!" cried Roo, terribly excited.

"Is that so?" said Eeyore, getting caught up by a little eddy, and turning slowly round three times. "I wondered."

"I didn't know you were playing," said Roo.

"I'm not," said Eeyore.

"Eeyore, what are you doing there?" said Rabbit.

"I'll give you three guesses, Rabbit. Digging holes in the ground? Wrong. Leaping from branch to branch of a young oak-tree? Wrong. Waiting for somebody to help me out of the river? Right. Give Rabbit time, and he'll always get the answer."

"But Eeyore," said Pooh in distress, "what can we – I mean, how shall we – do you think if we –"

"Yes," said Eeyore. "One of those would be just the thing. Thank you, Pooh."

There was a moment's silence while everybody thought.

"I've got a sort of idea," said Pooh at last, "but I don't suppose it's a very good one."

"I don't suppose it is either," said Eeyore.

"Go on, Pooh," said Rabbit. "Let's have it."

"Well, if we all threw stones and things into the river on one side of Eeyore, the stones would make waves, and the waves would wash him to the other side."

"That's a very good idea," said Rabbit, and Pooh looked happy again.

"Very," said Eeyore. "When I want to be washed, Pooh, I'll let you know."

But Pooh had got the biggest stone he could carry, and was leaning over the bridge, holding it in his paws.

"I'm not throwing it, I'm dropping it, Eeyore," he explained. "And then I can't miss – I mean I can't hit you. Could you stop turning round for a moment, because it muddles me rather?"

"No," said Eeyore. "I like turning round."

Pooh dropped his stone. There was a loud splash, and Eeyore disappeared ...

And then, just as Pooh was beginning to think that he must have chosen the wrong day for his Idea, something grey showed for a moment by the river bank ... and it got slowly bigger and bigger ... and at last it was Eeyore coming out.

With a shout they rushed off the bridge, and pushed and pulled at him; and soon he was standing among them again on dry land.

"Oh, Eeyore, you are wet!" said Piglet, feeling him.

Eeyore shook himself, and asked somebody to explain to Piglet what happened when you had been inside a river for quite a long time.

"How did you fall in, Eeyore?" asked Rabbit, as he dried him with Piglet's handkerchief.

"I was BOUNCED," said Eeyore.

"Oo," said Roo excitedly, "did somebody push you?"

"Somebody BOUNCED me. I was just thinking by the side of the river – thinking, if any of you know what that means – when I received a loud BOUNCE."

"Oh, Eeyore!" said everybody.

"But who did it?" asked Roo.

Eeyore didn't answer.

"I expect it was Tigger," said Piglet nervously.

"But, Eeyore," said Pooh, "was it a Joke, or an Accident? I mean –"

"I didn't stop to ask, Pooh. Even at the very bottom of the river I didn't stop to say to myself, 'Is this a Hearty Joke, or is it the Merest Accident?' I just floated to the surface, and said to myself, 'It's wet.' If you know what I mean."

"And where was Tigger?" asked Rabbit.

Before Eeyore could answer, there was a loud noise behind them, and through the hedge came Tigger himself.

"Hallo, everybody," said Tigger cheerfully.

"Hallo, Tigger," said Roo.

Rabbit became very important suddenly.

"Tigger," he said solemnly, "what happened just now?"

"Just when?" said Tigger a little uncomfortably.

"When you bounced Eeyore into the river."

"I didn't bounce him."

"You bounced me," said Eeyore gruffly.

"I didn't really. I had a cough, and I happened to be behind Eeyore, and I said 'Grr-oppp-ptschschschz'."

"That's what I call bouncing," said Eeyore. "Taking people by surprise. Very unpleasant habit."

"I didn't bounce, I coughed," said Tigger crossly.

"Bouncy or Coffy, it's all the same at the bottom of the river."

"Well," said Rabbit, "all I can say is – well, here's Christopher Robin, so he can say it."

Christopher Robin came down from the Forest to the bridge, feeling all sunny and careless, and just as if twice nineteen didn't matter a bit, as it didn't on such a happy afternoon.

"It's like this,
Christopher Robin,"
began Rabbit,
"Tigger –"

"All I did was I
coughed," said
Tigger.

"He bounced,"
said Eeyore.

"Well, I sort of boffed," said Tigger.

"Hush!" said Rabbit, holding up his paw.
"What does Christopher Robin think about it all?
That's the point."

"Well," said Christopher Robin, not quite sure
what it was all about. "I think –"

"Yes?" said everybody.

"I think we all ought to play Poohsticks."

So they did. And Eeyore, who had never played it before, won more times than anybody else; and Roo fell in twice, the first time by accident and the second time on purpose, because he suddenly saw Kanga coming from the Forest, and he knew he'd have to go to bed anyhow.

So then Rabbit said he'd go with them;
and Tigger and Eeyore went off together, because
Eeyore wanted to tell Tigger How to Win at
Poohsticks; and Christopher Robin and Pooh and
Piglet were left on the bridge by themselves.

For a long time they looked at the river beneath them, saying nothing, and the river said nothing too, for it felt very quiet and peaceful on this summer afternoon.

"Tigger is all right, really," said Piglet lazily.

"Of course he is," said Christopher Robin.

"Everybody is really," said Pooh. "That's what I think," said Pooh. "But I don't suppose I'm right," he said.

"Of course you are," said Christopher Robin.